Creepies

Jumble
Joan

Rose Impey
Illustrated by Moira Kemp

BARRON'S

NEW YORK

In my grandma's house
there's a dark and dusty attic.
I never go there
on my own.
But one day
my friend Mick and I
took my little sister there
— to frighten her.
It was Mick's idea.

After dinner
while Grandma was having a nap
we took my sister
by the hand
and climbed the stairs.

At the top I whispered,
"Do you dare to go in?"
And Mick said,
"I dare if you dare."

So I turned the handle,
the door creaked open,
and we tiptoed in.

The room was full of old things
in boxes and bags
and heaps on the floor.
And in the middle was a
tall brown rocking horse
with big teeth
and staring eyes.

"Shall we give her a ride?" I said,
and I winked at Mick.
But Mick said,
"Oh, I wouldn't,
if I were you.
It looks to me
like one of those
Ten O'Clock Horses."

"Ten O'Clock Horses?" I said.
And Mick said, "At night
when it's dark
and you can't get to sleep,
listen very carefully
when the clock strikes ten.
You'll hear the gallop
of horses' hooves.

"Then you must close your eyes
— don't dare to peep —
because if you do
you'll see
The Ten O'Clock Horses
breathing on your window,
watching you.

"And if they should
catch you awake
they'll come crashing in
to snatch you up
out of your nice warm bed,
and carry you off
into the cold, dark night."

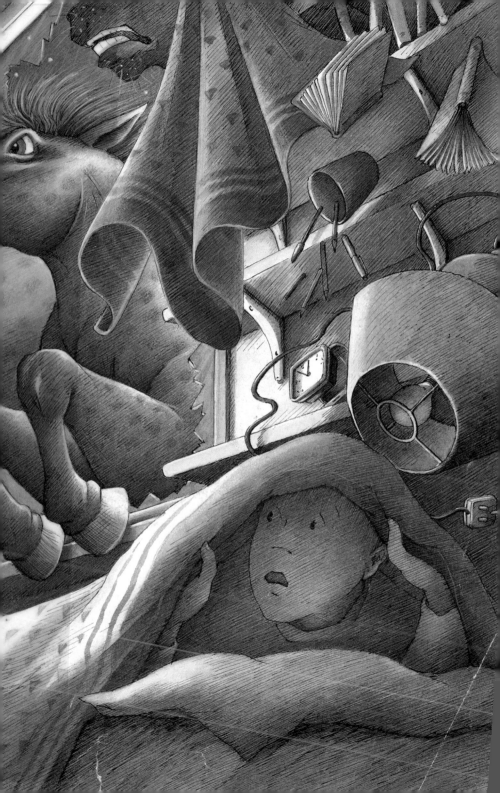

As we stood there
watching that horse,
watching us,
with its staring eyes,
it suddenly rose up into the air
and came CRASHING down,
its mouth wide open
ready to bite us.

Mick and I jumped back
out of the way
just in time.

"Come away from there," I said to my sister.
"Do you want it to bite you?"
Sometimes it's a good thing I'm there
to look after her.

Next Mick spotted a huge cage
covered with a cloth.
It looked as if something
was sleeping inside
and didn't want to be disturbed.

"You'd better keep away from there," I said,
"or else . . ."
"Or else . . . what?" asked Mick.
"Or else The Deadly Vampire Bat
might get you."

"Vampire Bat?" said Mick.
"Yes," I said. "For over a hundred years
it has lived in that cage.
As long as it's kept
completely in the dark
it's quite harmless.

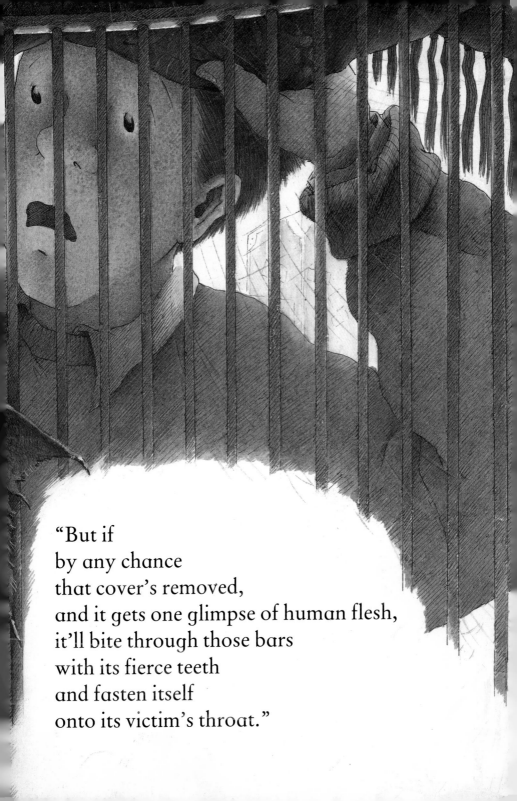

"But if
by any chance
that cover's removed,
and it gets one glimpse of human flesh,
it'll bite through those bars
with its fierce teeth
and fasten itself
onto its victim's throat."

Mick looked suspicious,
but I could see him
watching that cage,
just in case it moved.
And then it did!
It started to shake
as if something inside
was waking up.

Slowly the cover began to slip.
Mick and I backed away
bumping into each other.

We almost screamed
— but we didn't.
We don't scare that easy!

It was only a stuffed parrot,
full of moth holes.
Mick and I didn't think it was funny,
but my sister laughed.

"Come here," I said,
and I took her hand.
"I'd better keep my eye on you."

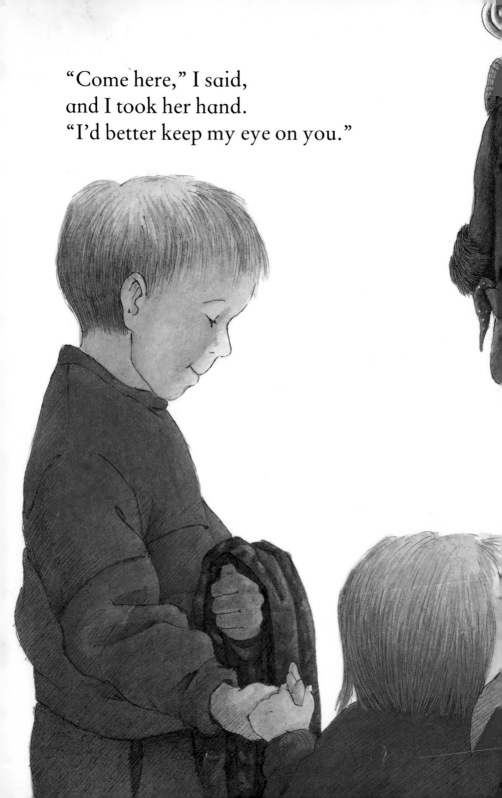

It was too late though.
My sister had spotted the wardrobe.
She wanted to play dressing up!
But Mick soon put a stop to that.
"You'd better watch out," he said,
"or Jumble Joan might get you."

"Jumble Joan?" I said.
So Mick winked at me.
"She's a horrible old woman
who kidnaps little children," he said.
"Little girls mostly," I said,
"with fair hair and blue eyes."

"She hangs up," said Mick,
"soft and lumpy
in dark cupboards
and deep wardrobes . . ."
"In attics," I said.
". . . pretending to be
nothing but a harmless set
of old clothes.

"When it's quiet
and just getting dark
she drops down
onto her fat rubbery legs
and wobbles out,
in search of
little girls to steal."

"When you least expect it," I said,
"she'll shuffle up
behind you,
drop to the floor
and lie quite still."

"Little by little," said Mick,
"so you hardly
see her move,
she'll edge
closer and closer.
Then . . . quick as a flash
she'll grab you
and stuff you
inside her great big skirts."

"No matter how much you scream," I said,
"no one will hear you;
you'll be trapped.
She'll carry you
struggling
back to her dark, dingy den."

It was cold in the attic now
with the wind blowing in
through the skylight.
And it was getting dark.

The clothes hanging around the wardrobe door
began to rustle and move.
The empty arms of coats
seemed to wave at us.
Mick and I looked at each other.
We didn't say anything
but we started to move,
very slowly at first.

Right behind us,
in the middle of the floor,
we saw a great heap of clothes.
It lay there soft and lumpy
blocking our way to the door.
"Mick . . ." I whispered, pointing.
And Mick nodded.

As we stared at it
we could see
two little eyes peeping out
from layers of skirts
and scarves and sweaters,
watching us.
Carefully,
without taking our eyes off it
for a minute,
we tiptoed
in a huge circle
right around the room.

When we were almost at the door
and Mick was reaching out
for the handle
the mountain rose up,
rushed forward,
and tried to grab us.

"Gotcha!" it said.

But it hadn't.
Mick and I
didn't waste a second.
We were off
— out of that door
and down those stairs,
as fast as greased lightning.
We didn't wait for my sister.

"She can look after herself."